His Dirty Secret

Book 4

Mia Black

Table of Contents

Prologue

Darius

"I could see myself with her," I muttered with my head resting against the counter of the bar. The bartender handed me another shot glass. I gulped it down, and I could see from the corner of my eye Jamar shaking his head.

"Slow down on the drinks," he advised me, but I wasn't listening. I needed something to help me. I was stressing out, and the drinks were helping out a little bit. He started laughing, looking at me struggle to get up. "Who do you see yourself with, Darius?" He was still laughing. "Be with who? Are you talking about Jayla? She's cute and all, but you have a wife, remember," he mumbled to me as he grabbed his drink. He took a sip of it and looked back at me.

"I love my wife," I confessed, slurring because of all the alcohol I was drinking. "I love Jayla too," I added. "What if I can't choose?" I asked him, still leaning on the counter for support. "I can just have both, right?"

My friend looked at me, shaking his head. I guess I looked pretty bad and pathetic right now.

"What can I tell you, man? There is no such thing as having them both!" He told me what I already suspected. "You can either have one or the other, but you can't have them both."

"Yes I can. I can have them both!" I argued. "Why can't I? They both want me, and I want the both of them. So by those rules I can have them both," I slurred some more and signaled for another drink. When I saw the bartender look over at Jamar, shaking her head, I knew that I was in worse shape than I thought.

"What do you want?" Jamar questioned me as he sipped his drink.

"What do I want?"

"Yeah. What do you want from them? There has to be something that one of them is giving you that the other isn't."

"Yeah?"

"So what is it?"

"I don't know."

"What is it about Jayla?"

"She cute."

"I know." He sighed. "But what else about her?"

"She's got a good head on her shoulders, she's strong, she's all about her family, and the sex." I sat up straight. "It's the best."

"And Shenice isn't?"

"I'm not saying that she isn't, but Jayla is something else when it comes to fucking." I smiled.

"And what about Shenice?"

"That's my wife, that's the mother of my child, and without her, I don't know where I would be. She pretty much gave me my career. She saw something in me that I didn't even know was there. I'm grateful to her."

"Being grateful and being in love are two different things."

"I know."

"And you should be fair to these ladies."

"I know." I started to get more annoyed.

"And one of these days you are going to have to choose."

"I know! I know! I fucking know!" I yelled.

The whole bar got quiet. Everyone was staring at me and I saw the bartender watching us. I ran my hand over my low-cut fade. I sighed and then breathed in hard.

"My fault," I apologized. I didn't mean to snap at Jamar, but he was asking too many fucking questions. The worst part about his fucking questions was that I didn't have the answers to them.

"It's alright." He took a deep breath while he settled the check. "I guess this shit is really stressing you out."

"It is."

"Well how about for now, you just do you." He stood up.

"What you mean?" I tried to stand, but I couldn't at the moment. Being the good friend that he was, Jamar helped me up.

"Alright, alright." He laughed as we made our way to the door. "You can have both, for now. Just watch out though. One of them is going to get tired of you. I can see it already."

I thought about what he said and shook my head. We left the bar.

Chapter 1

Jayla

Once again, I was at work. It seemed like I lived here more than I did at home. Coming here every day was starting to get depressing. I needed a break from this again.

"Is it me, or is this the longest day in history?" Charmaine asked me the second I got in the breakroom.

"It seems like that," I agreed. "It feels like ten hours has passed and it's only lunch," I complained.

"Tell me about it." She sighed.

"Are there no good men left?" Kim whined, plopping into a chair. She put down her personal pizza that she'd bought for lunch. Once we saw her pigging out, Charmaine and I knew that something was up.

Kim was a real careful and clean eater. Sometimes she ate junk food, but most of the time she was eating salads or veggies with meat. She was always watching what she ate. So to see her take a whole small pizza, and a pepperoni one at that, it was shocking.

"What is going on?" I asked.

"Yeah because if I'm not mistaken, this is you breaking your commandant. I thought you were trying to cut out all of the junk food this time," Charmaine added.

"You're not wrong."

"And what is this about men?" I was confused. "I thought you were just starting to date."

"Yeah, what's going on with that?"

"When I tell you guys this, you cannot and will not talk about this again." Kim started tearing off one of the pepperonis and put it into her mouth. "And I mean never again."

"What is it?"

She sighed and looked at us. The look on her face had me worried. What could it be?

"So I went on a date..." she started, sounding like she was talking about a funeral and not a date.

"Oh, isn't that suppose to be a good thing?" Charmaine shrugged her shoulders.

"You're right." Kim said. "It is suppose to be a good thing, but damn. It didn't turn out that way."

"Giiiiiiiiiiirrrrrrrrrlllll, will you stop dragging out this tea! I am here salivating waiting." Charmaine leaned in.

"Okay. So remember when I told you guys that I was going to start dating? I did. At first there was nobody out there that was really catching my eye. You know I got a type."

"Tall, light skin, built like a football player, with perfect teeth," Charmaine and I said at the same time, laughing.

"What you meant to say was funny, ambitious, and smart." She poked her tongue out. "And ya know me; I have a real emphasis on smart. So I started to talk to this guy, and the first red flag was that he didn't get a joke that I said. I thought maybe it was because it was a joke focused on something else or maybe he wasn't listening."

"What was the joke?"

"It was about a cook who was ordered to bake two whole chickens for her boss and his guest. She was so hungry after she finished baking them that she ate both of them. So when her boss and his guest got there, the boss went to sharpen his knives. The cook told the guest that he was sharpening his knives because he was really a cannibal and he planned on eating the guest's ears. The guest runs out the house, and then when the boss comes back, the cook tells the boss that the guest left with both of the baked hens. The cook runs after his guest with the knives screaming he wants just one, and the guest was crying holding on to their ears."

"That's messed up." I laughed. "The poor person thought they were going to lose their ears."

"You see? That's how a rational person gets the joke, but that's not what happened at all. He just kept going about what else the person could eat."

Charmaine and I exchanged looks.

"Wait a minute." She was holding back a laugh. "What do you mean?"

"He was like, so they were talking about the other food that they could eat?" Kim rolled her eyes. "And I'm trying to figure out if I even mentioned other food. Then he went on about what about giving them a salad, and I was just like, this is a fucking joke, not a life story or a suggestion."

"Wow." I laughed. "So he's not too bright is he?"

"No he is not. That was the first red flag, but I was thinking to myself that it was nothing and to not go into it. Then it got worse. We went on a walk because, you know, I told him that I like to walk, so he decided to come along. I thought that was cool and was a good thing. We get to a restaurant and he's like he's hungry and asks if we can go inside. I think cool, and then he said he didn't have any money on him."

"Noooooooooo," we both said to Kim, and she just shook her head.

"Yes. So I was going to be a good person and let it go. I ordered my food to go first and went to look out the window at something. He ordered his food, and then when it was time to pick up the food and tab, it was almost $30."

I looked over at Charmaine, and I swore she was about to pass out. She turned pale and looked like someone had stolen her soul.

"Giiiiiiiiiiirrrrrrrrrrrrrllllllllllllllllllllllll..." she stopped and took a breath. "No he didn't."

"Did he really buy the most expensive shit on the menu? On your dime?" I couldn't believe it.

"Yes he did." Kim sounded so ashamed. "I got up there and I was like, wait, how? I'm there about to argue with the lady, when she tells me what he ordered."

"What was it?"

"Crab legs, lobster, steak—" Kim started listing the items.

"Excuse me!" Charmaine coughed and almost died. She reached for her water and took a sip. "This shit almost killed me."

"How do you think I felt? He finally was like he ordered it, and when I said why did he order so much because there was no way I could help eat it all..." She drifted off and looked away.

"Damn. What did he say?" I wondered.

"He was like, he ordered the rest of the food for himself to eat the next day."

"Wait a minute!" Charmaine screamed. "That nigga broke too?"

We all busted out laughing. Nicki came by and told us to quiet down— we didn't want to wake up any of the residents—but it was too funny.

"What did he say that he did for work?"

"Oh, he was a businessman and that he owned his own business." She rolled her eyes.

"Giiiirrrrrrrllllllll, don't tell me that you fell for that."

"I did. I really did." She sighed.

"He must have been really good looking." I added, poking her with my elbow.

"Well...he really was." She giggled. "He looked like Trey Songz, just a shade lighter."

"Oooh." Charmaine shivered. "You already know I got a weakness for Mr. Songz." She smiled. "What else girl? Paint me a picture."

"And he had a body that could just throw you around with one hand."

"Mmm, you know I like them strong." I licked my lips.

"But it was just too much. After that, I cut him off, and then of course that's when the real bullshit starts."

"You mean it gets worse?" Charmaine gasped. "Girl, I was honestly not ready for all this tea that you are giving me, but I'm still sipping. Go ahead and tell it."

"He told me when he met me that he had no children."

"He has a kid?" I asked.

"He has several of them," she told us. "From several different women. I guess one of them found out about me, and even after I finished with him, she found me and told me the real. I'm talking about, I'm walking down the street and she came up to me."

"Oh no. He got himself some stalking women?" Charmaine looked at us while she asked. "That dick must be good too."

"I'm so glad that I never found out, because it turns out that he was a deadbeat, he never really worked, and he was a scammer. She was trying to warn me, but I was already gone."

"That's crazy," Charmaine said, shaking her head.

"Yeah it is," I added, but I felt a twinge of guilt.

My situation with Darius wasn't as dramatic as Kim's, but it wasn't the best situation ever. Although we are very much in love with each and we are going to be together exclusively, at the moment, he was technically married. I knew it was going to be a long process with this divorce. It was going to be a little bit of drama, but hopefully not that messy. I didn't want him tangled up in any nonsense. From what Darius told me, she could be a real bitch.

"So are you going back to not dating anybody?" I asked.

"Yeah are you going back to being a nun?" Charmaine winked. "Keeping that pussy to yourself?" We laughed.

"Basically it's going to be like that. My kitty is going to be locked down for a long time, or maybe forever."

"Forever?" Charmaine rolled her neck. "Girl, bye. You got to get someone in there to dust the cobwebs off every now and then."

"I can't get tangled up in no nonsense. If I meet someone great, then maybe I'll do that, but right now I'm not actively seeking anyone."

After work we all parted ways. Kim's story was still ringing in my head, and it just reminded me of my situation. I sighed and took out my phone. I was ready to read Darius's sweet message or to hear a nice voicemail from him. He was always leaving me something. It was nice to get off from work and know that someone was out there thinking about you as much as you'd been thinking about them. Darius was my sweetheart.

As I took out my phone and turned it back on, I waited for the notification sounds to go off. When I heard the text message sound finally go off, I smiled. Darius never disappointed me

"J, I'm starving. I thought you were going to get some groceries," a text message from Keon said. I looked at my phone and saw no phone calls or text messages from Darius. I felt empty. My phone vibrated.

"I was wondering when you were going call me. What's up boo?"

"I am not that lame nigga Darius," Keon told me. I could already see the mean look on his face. "You still with that lame ass?"

"Keon...let's not get into that now." I rolled my eyes. "What's up? Why are you calling me?"

"Did you get my text message?"

"I just got it now." I tapped into my Bluetooth and turned on my car. "What do you mean you're starving? I made you a home cooked meal and everything."

"I ate it all up." He sounded a bit suspicious.

"Ate it all up? How the fuck—" I cut myself off. "Who was in my house?"

"What do you mean?" He was trying to play dumb, but I wasn't having it.

"Keon, there is no way your ass ate all that damn food. I know you didn't have any trick in my house."

"J, how you even going to say that. You know I would never disrespect your house and bring some thirsty chick up in the condo. I had our cousin up in here, and you know that dude eat."

I closed my eye and remembered how many times I'd had to refill my fridge every time our cousin came over. I remember telling him the last time that if he came over, he had to put money toward the groceries.

"You're right." I sighed. "Alright. I'm going to go to the grocery store."

"Can you get some cake and—"

"Cut the sweets Keon. You are a grown ass man, aren't you? You stay, reminding me you a grown-ass man, and the first thing you are talking about is sweets," I teased.

"Whatever. I'm just bored."

"Why? You arm is much better. You can go out, you know."

"Yeah, but you know that I'm trying to stay out of trouble. I think it's best that I stay home."

I smiled hearing my brother say that. I didn't know if it was all the way genuine, but it was nice to hear that he was at least trying.

"That's good to hear. I'm really happy to hear that. How about I pick up something for you? You're being an adult."

"I'm a grown-ass man."

"I know." I sighed. "You always tell me."

Pulling up to the grocery store parking lot, I saw the whole strip of stores. There was a lingerie store at the end, a liquor store, the supermarket (of course), the bakery, and a hair salon/barber shop. I wanted to pick up an ultra sweet cake for Keon, but since the grocery store was closing soon, I decided to pick up the groceries first.

I must have went through every aisle of the grocery store. The cart was filled to capacity with items. I got fruit, dairy, meats, just everything to last the both of us for a long time. If Keon decided to invite our cousin over again, I had extra food just for him. I hoped he didn't invite him though, because it could get expensive with him around.

As I was walking toward the bakery, I saw someone that looked familiar. I squinted and looked closer. This woman looked like someone I knew. I couldn't put my finger on it. Before I went over there looking like a fool, I needed to try to remember where I'd seen her. The weird thing was, I didn't think I'd ever met her, but I knew for sure that I'd seen her. When I was a little closer, I finally really saw who it was. It was Shenice.

It was my first time really seeing her in public. I remembered once going to Darius's office and spotting her picture. I saw it quickly and saw how gorgeous she was. It would be easier to hate her if she was ugly, but she was not. Looking at her in person didn't help the whole situation. She was even more beautiful in person. I tried to hide myself, because I didn't know if she knew about me or not, but I was not willing to risk it. Hold up? Is that Darius?

Just then a tall man stood next to her, kissing her cheek. It was Darius. It had to be. This man was the exact same build as him. I really couldn't see his face because he had a cap on, but I knew that body well. I guessed this was the reason why he couldn't call or send me a text message. He was too busy playing perfect hubby to this fake-ass marriage. Or maybe it was my relationship that was fake. Maybe he's playing boyfriend with me and then he goes home and fucks his wife. I'm such a fucking fool.

I was ducking and hiding behind a car when I finally saw them go in. I took another look at that face under the cap and shook my head. Darius was such a fucking liar. Here he was with his wife, and then later he would be telling me that he loved me. He always wanted to go on and on about how I should trust him, but how could I when he lied to me? He could have just honestly told me that he was still in love with his wife and me at the same time. I wouldn't have stayed with him, of course, but at least then it would have been my choice to make. When he lies to me like this, he just makes all my decisions, leaving me in the dark.

I got a little bit closer, trying to get into the bakery and away from them, and as I got closer, I definitely recognized who it was. The guy with Shenice wasn't Darius at all. It was his best friend, Jamar. I damn near fell on the ground out of shock. I'd seen Jamar out with Darius, and if I'm not mistaken, he had slept with one of my friends. Damn, Jamar and Darius really looked alike. They could really pass as brothers because they looked so much alike. They were both drop-dead handsome men, and I guess Shenice liked Jamar too.

Ain't this a bitch? Here Darius was thinking of ways to break the news of the divorce to Shenice when she was out doing her own dirt. I ought to take a picture and send it to Darius. Sure, it would break his heart, but it just might speed up the whole process. He might see it, divorce her, and if she tried to pull anything in court, he would have the picture to show that she wasn't innocent either. This could solve everything. Who was I kidding? How could Darius even get mad at Shenice when he was basically doing the same thing? Shenice had Jamar and Darius had me.

Jamar and Shenice got into the car. The car pulled away and I went to the bakery. I ordered Keon's chocolate cake, and when I was about to leave, I ordered myself a bunch of brownies. I hated to admit that I was one of those girls that liked to stuff their face when they were upset, but right now, chocolate brownies would really hit the spot. Who knew doing this errand for Keon would turn into all of this?

On the drive back home, I couldn't get the image out of my head. The way he held Shanice's hand, the way he kissed her cheek, and just the whole thing was haunting me. But what I think haunted me the most was the way she smiled at him. She looked at him like he was her whole world. It was like that was the man of her dreams. This whole thing was so weird and so messy.

Speaking of messy, there was the car again. Jamar and Shenice were now at the gas station. They were cuddled up, leaning on the car, while the tank filled up. I slowed down my car to get a good look at them. I had to make sure that it really wasn't Darius. As I looked closer, I felt them looking back at me. I thought I was paranoid, but when I saw Shenice point at me, I knew they'd seen me. Jamar finished off at the gas station and closed the cap. They began walking toward my car, but I pressed on the gas and sped through the light just as it was turning red.

I look back at them in the rearview mirror. Shenice was pointing at me and Jamar had his hand on her shoulder. I shook my head at the whole situation. This thing was getting messier and messier. How the fuck did I end up here?

Keon was kicking back on the couch, watching reality TV. I knew he said that he was bored, but I didn't think it was that bad. He hated reality TV, because he thought the girls were just a bunch of nobodies thinking that they were somebodies. So when I saw him really into the TV program, I knew it had to be bad.

I tried to tiptoe past him because I didn't want him to see my face. I was still very shaken up by what had happened. I couldn't believe I had seen Jamar and Shenice. What was worse was that they had clearly seen me. I could pretend that they hadn't, but the fact that they'd been coming toward the car let me know that they had. I had to do something, but what? I couldn't tell Darius, because he and I were basically doing the same thing. I mean, he could be mad all he wanted, but that would be the pot calling the kettle black.

"What's wrong?' Keon asked, me standing up.

"The rest of the groceries are in the car." I put some of the bags on the kitchen counter. "I got you the cake that you like."

"That's cool," he said, "but I asked you a question." My brother was never one to let things go. I was a fool to think that he would start now. "What's wrong?"

"I don't know if I should tell you."

"J..." He drifted off. "What is going on?"

The look of concern in my brother's eyes warmed my heart. Ever since he'd been injured, we had gotten really close. Instead of us butting heads, we actually talked things out. This new Keon was being more rational. When he said earlier that he was trying to change, I could see it. When I used to come home before, the place would be a mess. It looked like a hurricane had been through the place.

But now that we were closer, he was neater. He would fix his bed, ask me about my day, or even help out around the condo. I knew that him staying with me was temporary, but the more I thought about it, I think I wanted him living with me forever.

For a long time, Keon had just been running wild and crashing wherever he could. Recently, he'd lived with one of his knucklehead friends. When he was out there, that was when I used to get so scared. I didn't know what he was doing or who he was with. Talking to Keon back then was like talking to a brick wall; there was no point. It was so frustrating. That was why it had been such a relief and blessing having him home with me. He was so much more level-headed now. He wanted to do more with his life, and I was proud of him.

"Sis, what's going on?" he asked me. I didn't want him to be in the middle of this mess. It was too much. But I knew nothing was going to be same again. Shit had just hit the fan.

"I'm so screwed."

Chapter 2

Jayla

The last few days, I really just kept to myself. After the whole thing with Shenice and Jamar, I'd just been going to work, coming home, and crashing on my couch. I didn't even go out with Charmaine and Kim, which to them meant that I was really sick. I just played it off and told them that I wanted to hang out with Keon, but that wasn't true. Even with Keon, I wasn't the same. We were talking, but I wasn't really listening. A part of me was still back in my car, at the gas station, watching Jamar and Shenice walk toward my car.

My phone was blowing up, but when I saw it wasn't my friends or Keon, I just let it go to voicemail. I'd been so to myself that I hadn't even bothered to check up on Darius. I knew that if I talked to him, that there was a chance I would tell him what I'd seen. I thought it was best just to avoid it all. I had to keep to myself. This mess was getting me depressed.

Keon came into the house with some groceries in his hands. He put my car keys on the hook and started to put the groceries away. He said something to me, but I really didn't hear him. I heard his voice but didn't hear any words. It was almost as if I'd gone deaf or something. He was looking at me, but I couldn't' really open my mouth. It was weird. I felt like I was trapped, but I didn't know how to get out.

"Jayla!" Keon was suddenly in front of me.

"Huh?" was all I managed to get out.

"Where were you?" he asked. "I was talking to you and you were just dazing off into space."

"Oh yeah?"

"Yes!"

"I heard you," I lied.

"Ok, then what did I say?" he crossed his arms, squinting at me. I chuckled and shook my head.

"What did you say?" I gave in. There was no point in me pretending that I had heard what he'd said. He'd already caught me.

"I was thanking you for letting me use your car."

"Oh okay. That's no problem. It's no big deal."

"No big deal?" he repeated back to me. "Did you forget that you said I would never touch your car because you were afraid I was going to crash it or somethin'?"

"I did?" I tried to remember. "I guess that sounds like something I would say."

"Yes, you did say that." His arms were still crossed. He squinted his eyes at me again. "Okay sis, what's going on?"

I sat up. I tried to come off as innocent. Before I opened my mouth, Keon put up his hand to stop me.

"Let me hold you up right there. Don't you open your mouth to tell me no bullshit either," he started. "Don't forget that this is your brother you're talking to. So if you're going to tell me something, I'm going to need you to be all the way honest, okay?"

"I don't know what you're saying."

"Jayla, what did you mean when you said the other night that you were screwed?" he asked. "Because it seems that ever since that night, you've been moping around the house. Look at you." He looked me up and down. "You got sweats on and your hair is a mess. You always use to make sure that you looked great at all times. What's going on sis? Let me know."

"I'm probably overreacting." I shrugged off. "Let's not make this a big deal."

"Make it a big deal? You let me be the judge of that," he told me.

"I really don't want to get into it." I tried to shrug it off again, but he was still standing firm. "Nothing is wrong, okay?"

"I don't believe you."

"I'm not—"

"I told you earlier sis, to not tell me any bullshit. So tell me what's going on?"

My brother was not budging on this one. He was in my face and he was very concerned. There was no way I would be able to tell him any little thing. If I was going to tell him, I had to tell him exactly what I'd seen. I couldn't filter it out at all.

"Well I was just at the grocery store..." I started the whole story. "And I happened to see someone."

"Who? You saw one of your friends?" he asked.

"No." I shook my head.

"Then who was it?"

"I saw Shenice," I told him.

"Who?"

"Shenice," I repeated again, but he still looked just as confused.

"Shenice? Who is Shenice? Is she an old friend, a coworker, or someone I should know? You've never talked about Shenice before."

That's when it hit me, about how much I'd left out about Darius. Keon already hated Darius, but this was going to make him go crazy. I thought about not telling him, but I'd already started to tell the story. There was no turning back now.

"Shenice is Darius's wife."

"His what?"

"His wife," I told him again, this time looking at the ground. He was so silent that I had to look up to see what he was doing.

"I knew it!" he exclaimed. "I knew that nigga was on some bullshit. He's such a piece of shit."

"Keon—"

"No, sis. Don't you start trying to defend him! I told you that nigga wasn't shit, and look, I was right." He paused and then looked at me. "When did you find out that he was married?"

It got quiet again and I went to the kitchen. I looked through the cabinets. If I was going to tell this whole story, I needed to drink something. It didn't need to be strong, but it had to be enough to get me through the story without breaking out in tears. I found an unopened bottle of pinot grigio. I got a small glass, opened the fridge, put in some ice cubes, and poured until it hit the brim. I popped the bottle in the freezer. I took a sip and then took a deep breath.

"I've known for some time that he was married."

"You mean to tell me that you willingly started to fuck some married guy?"

"It's not like that Keon. It's more complicated than it seems."

"Then what is it?"

"When I met him, he didn't tell me he was married."

"Typical of him."

"I found out later."

"He told you?" He crossed his arms.

"Not exactly.

"What the fuck is 'not exactly'? Either he did or he didn't. How did you find out?"

"His wife popped up one night."

Keon grabbed the cup from me and gulped down the rest. I was about to jump in that he was too young for alcohol, but in this situation, I was going to let it slide. After he put the drink down, he motioned for me to go on.

"Keep going."

"His wife came one night and he told me to hide out."

"Of course he did." He shook his head. "You do know that if it wasn't for the wife popping up he would have been glad to fuck you and her at the same time, right? He was going to keep that a secret from you for as long as he could."

"I don't think so."

"You're smarter than this Jayla." He sighed. "And he got you to be his side chick?"

"I am not his side chick."

"You not? He got a divorce from his wife?"

"He is getting one," I told him. "He went to file papers."

"Did she get served?"

"I don't know."

"Did you see the papers?"

"No, not really."

"Did he move out of the house? Is he not living with her anymore?"

"I don't know." I sat on the couch. "I don't think so."

"He's still with her Jayla."

"Divorces take time Keon."

"I'm sure they do, but that's no reason to still be living with his wife."

"She's not an easy woman to be with. He's always telling me stories—"

"You're better than that. Of course he's going to tell you stories about how she's a bitch. You think he could really tell you that he was with a wonderful woman? He can't say that shit because it wouldn't make sense that he was leaving her. He got to make himself look like the victim."

"Why would he do that?"

"That's part of the game. That nigga is playing you."

Keon was hitting all points. I didn't want to think that he was telling the truth, but I couldn't pretend that there wasn't truth in his words, either. He was right about so many things, but I loved Darius and I knew that he loved me.

"So what happened at the supermarket? What is it you trying to tell me? You saw his wife. What's the big deal about that?"

"It's not that I saw her. It's who I saw her with."

"Did you see her with her loving husband?" He smirked. I shook my head and avoided his teases. I knew he wanted to start an argument, and I really wasn't in the mood. I just had to let this story off my chest.

"No. I saw her with Darius's best friend. I saw her with Jamar."

Out of nowhere, Keon burst into laughter. He cracked up like I was a top-notch comedian and I'd told him my best joke. He even held his sides while he was laughing. I didn't think anything was funny at all. This would really hurt Darius. If he found out that his wife was messing around with his best friend, he just might go crazy. I wouldn't blame him at all.

"That's not funny." I crossed my arms at him this time. "It's not funny at all Keon." I playfully pushed him so that he would stop laughing.

"How is this not funny sis? That nigga Darius thinks he so fucking slick. He thinks he can fuck you and his wife at the same time. He thinks he can have the best of both worlds and that he is untouchable. I bet if you let him and if his wife let him, he would make you a sister wife and move you into the crib with them. I put nothing past that man at all." He shook his head. "What's happening to him right now is karma. You know people have always said that karma is a bitch."

"Karma?" I asked him.

"Hell fucking yeah it's karma." He laughed some more, even louder "What? You don't think this is the first time he's cheated on his wife? And I know you don't think you're the only other woman that's with him?" he pointed out.

Hearing Keon say those words about Darius being with someone else made my heart feel heavy and sad. There was no way Darius was seeing another woman besides me. When Darius wasn't at work, he was either with me or calling me. He couldn't possibly have the time. But Keon did have a point. If Darius could hide a wife from me for that long, who knew what else he was hiding? He might have another woman or anything else, but I couldn't think like that. I had to have faith in him. I loved him and that was all that mattered. If he said we would be together, I had to be patient.

"No he doesn't. Darius loves me," I informed him. "And I love him. I know that he's not sleeping around with anybody else, just like I'm not sleeping with anybody else."

"Whatever Jayla," Keon snapped back at me.

"So anyway, back to my story. I saw Shenice out with Jamar. While I was scoping them out, they saw me watching them."

"Does Shenice know what you look like?"

"I don't think so. I know Jamar knows who I am. I've been out with him and Darius before, plus he hooked up with one of my friends. So I know for sure at least one of them knows what I look like. Then they started to walk to the car and I drove off.

While I was driving away, I saw them pointing at my car."

"Damn. That is crazy."

"Yeah. I was thinking of telling Darius what I saw."

"Why? You think if he finds out that his wife is creeping with his friend, that will make him divorce her?"

"He's already divorcing her." I'd let him in on that secret. "This is just something I thought he should know, but I chickened out and haven't told him yet. I've even been avoiding him because I didn't want to chance that I'll blab about it. That's why I've been here to myself."

Keon shook his head again. Even he couldn't believe the mess. I think what made him a bit more disappointed was that I was somehow in this mess too.

"You know what?" He took in a deep breath and exhaled. "I think you did the right thing," he told me. "It's smart that you didn't tell Darius." His reply shocked me. I almost expected him to be laughing or cracking jokes some more.

"Why is that?" I was curious to know where his mind was.

"Because as much as you think you know, you really don't know the whole situation. This whole thing is nothing but bullshit. There is no reason for you to make it even messier. Weren't you the one always telling me that what's done in the dark doesn't stay there for long? Or something like that. When it's meant to come out, it will."

"I don't know. This seems like something I should tell him."

"Nah." He leaned back on the couch. "I mean, coming from you he might think you are just making it up. You did the right thing. Keep your mouth shut."

"Ok."

I started to feel a little better. It was good that I'd gotten this out. It had really been driving me crazy, but what was even crazier was that Keon was the one to make me feel better. It was nice that I could turn to him for this. I got up and began to cook dinner.

"And Jayla, because I'm your brother, I'm going to tell you to stop messing with him. Darius comes with a lot of bullshit. You already had some crazy shit with your ex. You can't leap from one fucked-up situation to another fucked-up situation. You need to leave him alone."

"Come on Keon, it's not even that serious." I tried to laugh it off. "I hear what you're saying, but believe me when I tell you that Darius is in love with me. As soon as his divorce is final and you see us together, you'll know that I'm not making this shit up. We're really going to be together and this will all be in the past. It may be a little crazy now, but once it's all said and done, I will be his wife," I let him know.

"Yeah, okay." He chuckled, walking away from me.

I turned around and continued to make dinner. Keon didn't know what he was talking about. He may have been right about some things, but he was wrong when it came to me ending up with Darius. I would have my man all to myself pretty soon. Once this divorce was final and all the dust settled, it was just going to be me and Darius. Keon would learn to love him and Darius would be the great big brother that he needs.

"I am going to be his wife," I whispered to myself.

Chapter 3

Jayla

More days passed and I was still ducking and dodging Darius. He even came to my job, and I told him quickly that I was busy with work. He tried to ask me what was going on, but I rushed him out. I felt guilty because I was so in love with him, but it was still kind of weird. The image of Shenice with Jamar was very fresh in my head. As I sat home on the couch again for another night, I thought about just biting the bullet. I had to call Darius. Not only did I miss him, but I owed him more than avoiding him. I loved him and he didn't deserve to be treated like this.

Just when I was about to call him, Darius called me first.

"I was just about to call you," I beamed, and when I heard him scoff, I knew that he was a little bit mad. Not that I could blame him for that though.

"Now why is it that I don't believe you?" he questioned. "I haven't heard from you in so long."

"I told you that I was busy with work."

"You've always been busy, but you've never been too busy to not see me or even talk to me. What's going on? What's new?"

"What do you mean, 'what's new?'"

"What I'm trying to say is that something new has to be going on for you to be ignoring my calls and texts. Something had to have happened. Is it Keon?"

"No, it's not Keon."

"Is something wrong with your sister? Is everything okay?"

"She's fine. You know she's almost ready for college, but nothing is wrong with her."

"Then what is it?"

I was tempted to tell him about what I'd seen. I wanted to scream that his wife was not only cheating on him, but she was cheating on him with his friend. But when I opened my mouth to say it, I remembered Keon's words. I didn't know the whole situation. I could only guess about what I'd seen. Even though it was a bad thing, I kept my mouth shut. If what Keon said was right, Darius would find out anyway. And maybe it's best that it didn't come from me.

"Just work babe, I promise. I told you how my supervisor can be a bitch, and she's really been on one lately. I just keep to myself because she is stressing me the fuck out. I didn't want to be around you and bring negative energy. I know you get enough of that type of bullshit at your house. I know you are stressing right now with this whole divorce thing, so I was just going to cool down from my supervisor's antics, and when I felt like myself, I was going to contact you. I'm sorry if you felt neglected or like I was trying to play you, but in all honesty, it wasn't about you. I love you."

I heard him sigh. I could feel him think about what I had just said. It was quite the long pause, but soon he spoke.

"I get it. Sometimes my work can make me just not want to be around anybody. I respect the way your mind thinks. Most people, when they go through something negative, they want to drag everyone around them down. It's nice to know that the woman I love is so considerate."

"Are you smiling?"

"Yeah, I am." He chuckled.

"I can tell."

We started talking and laughing like old times. It felt good to talk to him again. It really showed how much we missed each other, because we were going nonstop. He had me cracking up about one of his clients.

"So I tell the lady that we can get her a huge brick house and it will be in a great neighborhood. I drive her out there and bring her to this beautiful home. Jayla, the place was great. It had huge windows, great lighting, a working fireplace in three rooms, and it even had a Jacuzzi out back. For the price it was listed for, it was so outrageous. It was so affordable that anyone could buy it." He started to share.

"This woman looks at the house, and the whole time she is frowning. I ask her what's going on and why does she have such a long face. She finally tells me that she isn't that crazy about the material of the house. Now I'm thinking, it can't be the brick, because she was so firm about the house being a brick house, so I'm naming every other material. Then I ask her straight out: Is it the brick that you don't like? And she tells me yes. When I remind her that she was the one who wanted brick, she says yes, but not this type of brick. She wanted a specific color. To make a long story short, she was really talking about wood and not brick. I've never been so mad about all the time I wasted. She was calling me day and night, talking about brick this and brick that, and when I get her to a brick house, she doesn't like brick anymore."

I started laughing. Darius joined in too. I loved when he told me about his clients. It made my job look a little better.

"I missed you," he told me out of nowhere.

"I missed you too."

"I needed this. I needed you," he added, and I smiled on my end of the conversation. "Can I see you tonight, or are you still in a bad mood?" I hesitated for a bit. "What is it? Are you still not up to seeing people?"

"It's not that." I didn't want to tell him about Jamar and Shenice, so I had to be careful. I had to do my best to not say a word. "I'd love to see you tonight. I'm missing my man." I gave him a seductive laugh.

"So I'll come and see you tonight for dinner?"

"Sure."

The second the conversation was over, I leaped into the shower to get ready for work. I was so glad that Keon had gone over to our cousin's house for a bit. I didn't need him here giving me the same speech and lecture about Darius. I was in love with him and he was in love with me. When we get together, it was like magic. It was like we were made for each other. I'd never been the type of girl to believe in soulmates and the one type bullshit, but I'd be lying if I didn't say I thought Darius was the one for me. He was the one for me and the last one that would ever have me.

At work, it was business as usual. I helped out my patients, filled out some forms, and looked forward to lunch. When I saw Kim and Charmaine gossiping in the break room, I knew it was going to be yet again another story.

"Giiiiiirrrrrrllllll," Charmaine said in the way that only she knew how. "Do I got some good tea for you."

"Ya'll two always got something to tell me." I laughed.

"And you listen every time too bitch, because you know you love it. You live for the tea and you love this shade girl." She whipped her head around. "First, do you like my hair? I got some new Malaysian bundles put in the other day."

"Oh did you?" Kim said while looking at her. "Is that why you keep flipping your head around?" She laughed. "You trying to reach for a compliment."

"A bitch can't feel good about herself?" Charmaine teased. "A bitch can't feel like Superwoman after she gets some bundles in her hair?"

"She can but, damn, with the hair flipping you looking like a shampoo commercial." Kim laughed some more and I joined in.

"Don't be a hater boo." She stuck her tongue out at Kim.

"Well it looks good on you," I told her truthfully. "I was going to say something nice about it before you opened your mouth." I laughed. "Now tell me this juice."

Charmaine was always dramatic. You'd think she was trying to get an Oscar or something. She was always building up the suspense. She looked at both of us for several minutes. She would stare at me and then turn to stare at Kim.

"Girl, if you don't start opening your mouth to tell us, I'm going to pull some tracks out." I reached for her hair. "Damn. This shit is soft," I pointed out.

"I know right?" Charmaine smiled. "Okay, so I was on a date with this guy, and before you say it Kim, it wasn't as bad as your date." We all laughed.

"Don't remind me." Kim rolled her eyes.

"The guy was cute and he was a gentleman, and he paid for dinner..." She looked over at Kim with a wink.

"Why are you over there trying to throw shade?" Kim chuckled.

"Because I can. But the date went well and we got to my place. So we ripping off our clothes—"

"Wait a minute. Was this the first date?" Kim asked.

"Yes? You are the only one playing a nun boo. But let's not forget the wild nights you had back in the day." We all smiled. "But he and I were ripping off each other's clothes, and when I expected him to give me the D, he went eating instead."

"You say that like it's a bad thing." I scrunched my face. "You don't like it when a man eats you out?"

"Girl, bye. I love that shit. And this guy, he ate my pussy like was starving. When I tell you that he painted my whole entire pussy with his tongue, that's exactly what he did. He didn't leave one spot untouched. He had me in there praising Jesus, God, Mary, Joseph, just everybody. I've never came so many times back to motherfucking back."

"Then what's the problem?"

She took a long sip of her water. She shook her head and held out her hands.

"You won't want to hear it. After he did all of that, I asked him to put it in."

"Oh yeah." Kim rolled her hips. "Damn girl, I'm going to have to get you a rabbit toy. I heard it makes a girl cum every time."

Charmaine nudged her with her shoulder. "No, but he pulled out, and when he even grazed my pussy, he came."

"What?" Kim and I said at the same time.

"Yes. The parts touched each other and he came. He took the condom off and then went inside. Two strokes later and he was coming again."

"You are lying," I said. "Two strokes."

"Yes, only two, and they weren't even that good." She sighed. "It wasn't like it was two good strokes and then he stopped. It was two barely strokes and he gave in. It was so bad. And then he couldn't get his dick hard. It was like I sucked on it, I jerked him off, and that shit was like a dead fish. It flopped and flopped."

We all just sank our shoulders. I hadn't had a situation like that. Charmaine looked like someone had tried to steal her joy.

"Then what happened?"

"I kicked him out. I told him to get his mediocre sex and floppy dick-having ass out of my apartment. He's lucky I let him get dressed." She looked at her nails.

"But you said he could eat you out real good," Kim added. "That wasn't enough?"

"No wench. I want it all. I want him to have a big, stiff dick and a nice, stiff tongue."

"Oh boy." I laughed.

"I got some news too," Kim said.

"Don't tell me you got back with that guy with all the baby mamas?" I joked.

"Hell no," she spat out, and Charmaine and I laughed.

"Then what is it?" Charmaine asked.

"I got a text from Darius's friend Jamar," Kim casually mentioned.

My heart almost leaped out of my chest. I didn't expect to hear that.

"Oh?" I was trying to sound cool, but I was really nervous.

"Yeah. It was so weird, because it came out of nowhere," Kim went on.

"I haven't ever heard you talk about him," Charmaine said. "I mean, besides that one time ya two hooked up, you never talk about him. Why is that?"

"What is there to say? We met in the club, exchanged numbers, fucked each other, and that was it. It wasn't like we fell in love or anything."

"Did you like him though?" Charmaine asked, and I leaned in to listen.

"He was cool, but even before we got together, we knew what it was. It was just going to be us having sex that one time. That's why I never went into details with you guys. There wasn't much to say."

"So what did the text message say?" I asked while my heart was still racing.

"He was just inviting us to go to the club with him," she told us. "He just wanted us to all hang out.

It was just a little weird seeing his number pop up and all."

"It can't be that weird." Charmaine winked. "You must have put it on him more than you know. Or maybe he wants to get you back into bed. He wants that old thing back, girl." She giggled.

"The other thing that was weird about it though, was that he kept hitting me up. Like he texted and called me almost nonstop. He was so desperate to reach me. At first I didn't pick up because I didn't recognize the number, but once the text messages started, it didn't stop there. I just thought that part was weird. It was like he needed to speak with me badly."

I gave a small grin. I didn't want to tell them what was going on. I'd let so much of the story out that I would have to catch them all up. I had already done that with Keon, and I wasn't ready to do that with them.

If only Kim knew that Jamar reaching out to her had nothing to do with her. I bet the only reason he had reached out to her was to get to me. He was trying to talk to me or at least get me in the same room with him. He probably wanted to see what I knew or if I had said anything to Darius. Or maybe he wanted to know whether or not I planned to tell Darius anything. He wanted to see me and he wanted to know what I was going to do with what I saw.

"So what did you tell him?" I casually asked.

"I told him no." Kim shrugged her shoulders and I felt relieved.

"What? Why?" Charmaine poked for more information.

"Because it was weird, and on top of that, let's not forget about the drama Darius put Jayla through. It just felt like it could be a messy situation."

"That whole shit with Jayla was so long ago. Jayla is way over that now. I'm just mad that you turned down free drinks."

"What do you mean by that, Charmaine?"

"Well you know that when a guy invites you out he's willing to pay for your food." She smiled but then it went away. "Oh I get it. The last dude got you paranoid about your coin. You got so used to paying for things, you don't want to chance it," she joked, poking fun at her last situation.

"Shut up." Kim laughed.

I laughed too, but it was all pretend. Although she had turned down his offer, the fact that he had made it worried me. What was the plan? Did he want to talk to me? Had he invited Shenice too? Was the plan to get me there so that the both of them could see me? I was glad that Kim had turned him down, but these questions would be in my head for a long time.

It was finally time to have dinner with Darius. I dressed my best and the sexiest that I could. I wanted him to drool the second he saw me. I missed him so much, and I loved how he looked at me. With my formfitting black dress, I stepped out of the condo. His eyes opened wide and he smiled just as widely too.

"It's almost unfair how good you look right now," he told me. I looked at him in his nice designer pants, shoes, and casual shirt.

"I could say the same to you." I reached up and kissed him softly on the lips. I went to pull away, but his arm was around my waist and he pulled me closer. He didn't let me go for a long time. What started off as an innocent kiss pretty soon turned into something that could be seen in a porn.

"Okay, let's try not to fuck right in front of my home please."

"You are the one that came out looking like that." He smiled. "But you're right. We have dinner reservations to make."

I almost burst out laughing when I saw that he had brought me back to my favorite restaurant. He knew how much I loved the steak here.

"You keep teasing me about the steak, but you never hesitate to bring me back to get some more." I laughed after he held out my seat.

"That' because I love you. You should see how much your face lights up every time we come here. I love to see it." He smiled at me so sincerely. I at first felt great, but then the image of Shenice and Jamar popped into my head. "Are you okay?" he asked.

"Oh, I'm fine." I played it off. "I am just so hungry," I commented.

"Are you hungry for just anything? Would you like to try something new here?" He was teasing me, but I didn't care.

"Now you and I both know that's not going to happen."

After we ordered, Darius caught me up with another story about the same client.

"So I finally got her to fall in love with a house. It's this beautiful townhome. It's bigger than the last home and even in her price range. The schools in the area are some of the best in Georgia, and it isn't that far from any shops or shopping malls. She says she loves it, she's about to come in and sign, and then guess what?"

"What?" I was already laughing a little bit.

"She then proceeds to tell me that she wants the original house she saw. She was no longer in love with the one that we had all the paperwork for. So now we have to do it all over again for the first house."

"You know what you should really do?" I chimed in. "What you should really do is get paperwork ready for both houses. Just do as much as you can, and if she pulls that mess, just switch it and force her to sign."

"That is so smart." He stopped. "Why didn't I think of that?"

"She sounds like she can't make up her mind."

"Evidently."

We started laughing again, and when I saw the waiter with our food, I got excited. He placed it in front of us. I bit into the succulent steak and damn near died. I didn't know how they did it, but every time I ate the steak, it felt like the first time. I had to meet the chef and thank him for all that he'd done. I was never disappointed when I came here.

Darius went on to tell me other stories and ask me about work. When I saw how attentive, loving, and caring he was being, it made me feel a bit guilty. Here he was being so nice to me and I hadn't even bothered to tell him what I knew. I should have told him about Jamar and Shenice. I knew he might say that I was overreacting, but it was just the way they were around each other. They were all lovey-dovey. She looked at him in a way that could never be mistaken for friendship. There was definitely something going on between those two.

"What is going on with you?" Darius asked.

"What do you mean?"

"You've been quiet at times during the evening. You've barely touched your food. And you can't tell me that you don't like it, because you and I both know how much you love this steak and this restaurant. What is going on?"

I should just tell him. He had a right to know. Even though he was not completely innocent, at least he hadn't cheated on her with a friend. It was crazy that Shenice would do that. I guessed he was right about her. He used to always say that she was a bitch, but, damn, I never thought it would be like this. I never thought that she would go after his friend. In fact, I didn't know who I am more disgusted by: Shenice for sleeping with Jamar, or Jamar for betraying Darius.

Darius has always said that he and Jamar were like brothers. Jamar dealt with the marketing of his real estate. He came up with concepts for their ads and how they promoted the company. He was one of the people who helped them become so successful. Darius loved working with Jamar. Even though Jamar was in and out of the office, he was always working hard. Darius respected that and him. He always spoke highly of him. It was going to break his heart to know that his friend was sleeping with his wife. I should just keep it to myself.

"Nothing is wrong," I assured him. "I just miss you. I can't believe it's been so long since we've seen each other."

"I know. I have to see you every day."

"I'm sorry," I apologized again. "You know how hectic work can get." I was going to ride this lie forever.

"I know what you mean. Right now work is getting so hectic. Jamar and I have a lot on our plates."

Hearing Jamar's name almost sent chills down my spine. I not only had the image of him and Shenice together, but I couldn't forget the fact that he had reached out to Kim. He had reached out multiple times in an effort to get to me.

"How long have you and Jamar known each other?"

"Practically our whole lives. I told you that he's like my brother."

"Right."

"In fact, I remember once when he and I tried to sneak a peek down the shirt of our teacher."

"What?" I laughed. "Such pervs."

"We were in junior high school, with so many hormones that we didn't know what to do with ourselves. So Jamar comes up with the brilliant idea of one of us faking an injury so that she could comfort us. Now there was one problem with this ingenious idea: we had to decide which one of us had to fake the injury. Then after a lot of back and forth, we thought it was best that one of us was really injured. Finally Jamar takes the loss and he trips himself to fall. He scrapes his knee really badly. She runs out and is about to hug him, but guess what happened?"

"You got in trouble because she figured you guys were doing something bad?"

"No. As soon as she saw the blood coming out of his knee, she passed out. She couldn't stand the sight of blood."

I chuckled a bit at the story. Had I never seen Shenice with Jamar, I knew I would have laughed harder.

"Come on, that's a pretty funny story," he boasted. "Every time I tell people that story, everyone busts out laughing.

"It's funny." I added a few more laughs, but he wasn't buying it.

"Jayla, are you sure that there is nothing going on?"

Once again I opened the mouth to tell him the truth, but I knew that it was going to do more harm than good if I was the one to reveal this secret. If he was going to find out, it wasn't going to be from me.

"No, I told you that I'm fine." I slowly kicked off my shoe and hiked my foot up his pants. It hit his crotch and he nearly jumped up. "What's the matter?" I slyly asked him after seeing his reaction.

"You're not too old to be playing footsies still?"

"Would you like me to stop?" I was now circling my foot softly around his crotch. He was getting hard to the touch. He closed his eyes a bit as I moved faster around it. He was enjoying it. He even opened his legs more.

"No. Don't stop," he told me softly. Hearing him being pleased of course turned me on. I looked around the restaurant and saw that nobody was looking at us. Luckily we weren't really around other people. After seeing that, I ducked underneath the table.

"Jayla?" He moved the long tablecloth to look at me, but I pulled it back down.

"Keep a lookout," I demanded him. I pulled him out swiftly. Seeing his rock-hard penis brought a smile to my face. I licked it up slowly and felt him squirm. I pinched his thigh, telling him to keep still. I then shoved him completely into my mouth and bobbed up and down as much as I could. I was so used to seeing his face when I did this, but there was something exciting about doing it like this. It thrilled me for some reason.

I sped up and he got even harder. I slowed down then and covered every part of him with my tongue. I remembered Charmaine talking about the guy painting his tongue all over her sex, so I did the same to Darius. I took my tongue and gave him long strokes up and down. I imagine that my tongue was a paintbrush and I had to make my masterpiece. I gave the base of him of firm grip and kept going until he started shifting more. This was usually the time that he came, and sure enough, seconds later he exploded.

"Is anybody looking?" I whispered after I fixed myself up.

"No. Come quick. They are singing happy birthday to someone on the other side of the room," he let me know. As soon as I heard the staff clapping, I got out and slipped back into my seat. No one noticed. I looked over at Darius, and he had this silly grin across his face. He looked exhausted, but only I knew why.

"What's wrong?" I sipped my wine slowly. "You looked drained." I worded it perfectly.

"I don't know." He played along. "It was as if all the energy was drained out of me. It came out of nowhere."

We both were chuckling, but now we both were horny.

"So how long before you take me somewhere and bend me over?" I asked.

"Oh, it's like that?"

"Don't act like you haven't been picturing me naked this whole time. You know you want to fuck me. You know you want to dive headfirst into my pussy."

"What else do I want?"

"You want to put yourself slowly inside me so you can remember how good I feel."

"You are right. I am thinking about that. It's good that you know me so well." He put his hand up and the waiter came right away. "May we please have the check? We have someplace to get to."

We went outside and waited for the valet to bring the car around. Suddenly Darius grabbed me around my waist and kissed me. It was so hot and passionate that when the valet got back, he had to get our attention.

"Thanks," Darius told the young man, and then he turned back to me. "I can't wait to get you alone."

"How about we find someplace close for just a little preview?" I kissed him again. "We can hop in the car again."

"No. I'm going to take you to a huge suite and do it right." He grabbed my ass, giving it a firm squeeze. "Because I know once I get started, I'm not going to stop." He kissed my neck.

We were leaning against the car, making out, when suddenly his phone vibrated. He groaned and pulled away from me.

"One second babe." He looked at his phone. "It's Jamar. Excuse me while I take this. It might be about work. Jamar has been going crazy about this new promotion campaign for the real estate company." He picked up the phone call. "What's going on Jamar?" He listened to what he said. "That's great, but if this is not about work, I'm going to call you back." He paused. "Yeah. It's just that right now I'm out with Jayla." He stopped again. "Yeah, Jayla. She's right next to me. Look, I'm going to call you later." I could hear the panic in the tone of Jamar's voice. I couldn't tell what he was saying, but I knew I heard how worried he sounded. "I'll call you later." Darius seemed to be trying to get off the phone. "Ok. Bye!" he finished. "Damn. I never had a problem letting go of Jamar off the phone before." He chuckled.

"I can believe that."

He opened the car door for me. I went to get in when I saw something familiar. I saw the same car that I had seen Jamar and Shenice in. It was on the other side of the street. Darius got in the car, but I was still staring at the other one. I was pretty sure it was the same car from that day.

"Is everything okay?" Darius asked. I shook my head. Shenice was not the only person in the world to have that car.

"Just taking in some air," I lied. I got in the car.

Chapter 4

Shenice

I sat in the car across the street, watching Darius get in the car with that slut. He had taken her to this restaurant that was known for their steaks. I guess that would explain why he'd thought I wanted a steak dinner that one time. He had really been confusing me with that little girl. Darius was such a piece of shit, but damn, I might have fucked up this time. I couldn't believe she had seen me and Jamar together.

This wasn't meant to happen. In fact, Jamar and I weren't even supposed to meet. I was just in the lingerie shop trying to find something sexy. I loved the way Jamar had looked at me last time when I'd showed him my last vixen outfit. He hadn't been able to get his eyes off me. I just wanted to buy something else for him. I wanted him to take me away and have his way with me.

Flashback:

My phone vibrated while I was shopping at the lingerie store. I smiled when I saw Jamar's name.

"Hey you." I giggled.

"What's up? What are you up to right now? Are you busy?"

"No, I'm not busy." I looked through a rack of lingerie clothes. "I'm just shopping while the baby is at her grandmother's. What are you up to?"

"I just finished a meeting. Hopefully this new thing will make the company even more money."

"My man is hard at work."

"You know it. But you know what I'm in the mood for right now?"

"What is it?"

"I would like to see you. Can I?"

"Of course, but I have to warn you about the place where I am. I don't know."

"You don't know what?"

"Let me just text you the address. I'll see you when you get here."

About fifteen minutes later, I spotted Jamar walking into the store. The smile on his face was funny. He was staring at the displays. There were bras, boy shorts, teddies, camisoles, sleeping gowns, bodysuits, and chemises. I expected him to look uncomfortable, like most men did when they stepped foot into this place, but he looked like he was okay. Maybe he didn't care where he was, or maybe it was the fact that the store was practically empty.

"Very interesting store selection." He smiled and pulled me in close. He kissed me and hugged me. He smelled so great, and I licked my lips. "It's so good to see you."

"It's good to see you too." I felt my heartbeat slow down. I was falling for Jamar hard.

"I thought that maybe you wouldn't want to see me."

"Why is that?"

"Because I know how you feel about us being seen in public."

Jamar and I were real careful about how we messed around. We usually went to a restaurant that was far away, to his place, or sometimes very rarely we went to a hotel room. It was nice being with him even though we had to hide it. But I guessed I got where he was coming from. Whenever he suggested that we do something new and out in the open, I told him flat out, no.

"Hey, you're the one that wanted to see me. If anything goes wrong, you can blame yourself," I teased him, pressing my body against his.

"So what are you doing here?" He looked around the lingerie shop. "What's the reason behind it?" He touched one of the mannequins and then looked back at me.

"I just wanted to get something sexy. You know, I was thinking of the last time I wore something sexy for you."

"This is for me?"

"Yes" I told him.

"So, shouldn't I have some say in it?"

"I guess you should."

"How about you try a few things on?"

I went toward the fitting room. I took a couple of outfits with me. The first one was this red lace bodysuit. It was completely see-through and extra tight. It hugged my body like a glove, and when I stepped out, Jamar's eyes almost popped out of his head.

"What do you think of this one?" I spun around so he could get a good look at me at all angles. He licked his lips but wasn't really saying anything. "You're not going to say anything?"

"Damn" was the first word he said. He was sitting down right across from the fitting room. He adjusted himself in his pants. "Got my shit hard." He laughed, pulling his pants down some more.

"Already?" I laughed. "You haven't even seen the other ones," I mentioned. "Some of them are really sexy. I don't think you can handle it."

"I can handle it. I know that you're going to look good in all of them."

"Well let me go try on the other one."

The white, open bra, crotch-less sleepwear was too sexy. My breasts poked out and stood firm. I wasn't use to being topless, but I loved what I saw.

"Um, this one looks great!" I yelled over the cloth door.

"Then come out and let me see you."

"I don't think I should walk out there."

"Why not? Nobody is out here." He paused. "Even the person that works here is glued to her phone, and it's not like you're by any windows."

"Ok." I shrugged my shoulders. "You have a point."

I walked out slowly. Jamar immediately stood up and walked toward me.

"Oh shit." He brought me back to the fitting room and closed the curtain behind him. "You can't step out there like that."

"This is why I was hesitant." I giggled. He wasn't really listening to me. He was still staring at my body. "Hello?" I snapped in his face. "Are you there?" I laughed.

"Huh?"

"Are you a bit distracted?"

"Just a bit."

"Don't you think that this room is a bit overcrowded?" I whispered.

He didn't answer me this time. He just picked me up and placed me on the bench. He bent me over, pushed my thong to the side, and started to lick me. He licked every hole, every inch, and every part of me. I was biting down on my tongue really hard. I didn't want to make a peep. We were still the only customers in here. The worker might be distracted, but I didn't want to take any risks. He wasn't going to make it easy for me at all. His tongue was putting in work.

"Jamar..." I moaned slightly, but I violently jerked around. My climax came raging out of me. My body twisted and turned all around. He caught me before I could fall on the ground and make any noise. I was panting. I was about to stand back up when he bent me over again. "What is it?" I asked him, and then I felt his hard dick press against my wet, aching hole. "Jamar."

"I just want to feel it," he told me, but I know he was lying. "You're so fucking warm," he breathed. He pushed a little bit of himself in and then came out. "And you're so fucking tight." He pushed a little more of himself in and then came out. "And so fucking wet." He pushed himself in and out of me again.

"Shit," I whispered.

"What's that? I didn't hear you." But I knew he was lying. It was all in the tone of his voice. He was enjoying the fact that he was teasing me. He knew I wanted him. My sex was pulsating and begging for it.

"Fuck me."

He dived into me. I whimpered and sighed. He felt so good. My palms were so sweaty, but I had to hold on. He was grabbing my hips, pulling me against himself, and playing with my nipples. He then grabbed my ass and dug his nails in. He loved getting a nice, firm grip on me. He knew that shit drove me crazy. My body temperature started to get nice and warm. My legs started to get wobbly and he was panting hard. He had to go fast because we didn't want to get caught. We didn't know what the salesperson was doing.

I threw my body back and he let go of my hips so I could do some of the work. He pulled my hair and went deeper in me. He pulled my head hard and placed his hand around my neck.

"Damn." I moaned. "You know I like that shit," I told him. He squeezed, and we both grunted against each other. Just when we thought we weren't going to make any more loud noises, we both finished.

"Ma'am?" the salesperson said from afar. "Are you okay? Do you need me to come back there and help you?" I could hear her walking over.

"No. It's okay!" I yelled back. "My hair got trapped in the zipper. My boyfriend was just helping me get unstuck." We started to fix ourselves up. "I'll be right out there. Jamar peeked out and then ran to sit down. I quickly got myself dressed. I snatched my hair into a smooth ponytail. I grabbed all the items and went toward the register.

"I'm going to buy all of these items." I smiled.

"That's great." She was so polite. She came across a store tag but no item. "Is this from something?" she asked. I smiled wider and started looking away.

"I'm wearing one of the items," I informed her, and she started laughing.

"I respect your honesty." She was still laughing. "Okay. Your total will be $185.30." She put all the items into a shopping bag.

"I got this." Jamar handed her a credit card.

"Wait—"

"I told you that I got this." He cut me off with a smile.

"Let your boyfriend spoil you," the worker said, putting in her two cents.

"Yes, let me spoil my girlfriend." His smile grew even wider. "Thank you." He signed the receipt and we left the store.

"Damn, you are spoiling me." I smiled, looking at him.

"I am?" He held on to the bags.

"Yes," I admitted to him. "I can't remember the last time I felt so good." I looked at him lovingly. I was about to reach up and kissed him, but I stopped. I thought I saw someone familiar hiding behind a car in the parking lot. I shook it off and we got into my car.

"What happened to your car?" I asked him.

"I left it at home. I've been taking cabs all day," he told me. "You not going to give me a ride?"

"Hmm..." I pretended to think about it. "The sex was pretty good." I kept playing around. "I guess the least I could do is give you a ride." I poked fun at him.

"Whatever." He laughed. "You got jokes, but you barely have gas in your car," he told me as I pulled out of the parking lot.

"Oh shit. I knew that there was something I'd forgotten to do." I sighed. "Fine. I'll just go to the gas station."

Jamar decided to fill up my cap. I didn't know why I found it sexy of him doing it for me. He didn't even hesitate, and I didn't even ask. The second we got in, he got out of the car and took his credit card out. I watched him and couldn't help myself. I exited my car and went up to him. I leaned him against the car, kissed him, and then wrapped my arms around him.

"What was that for?" he asked.

"No reason behind it. I just kissed you because you are you." I smiled. I hugged him again. I looked at the street and saw Darius's slut staring at me from her car.

"Oh shit."

I blinked my eyes to make sure, and it was really her. I could never forget the face of Darius's whore. She looked me and looked at Jamar.

"What is it?" he asked, and he turned around and saw what I was staring at. "Oh shit. Jayla," he said.

"Is that her name?" I asked. She was still looking at us. "I should go over there and say something to her."

"I thought you wanted to keep a low profile."

"I do, but I just have to say something to her." I started to walk, and Jamar came up behind me. We didn't even get to walk five steps before she peeled off. "Fuck!" I screamed and pointed at the car. "What the fuck are we going to do?"

Present:

That was then. When I saw the look in that girl's eyes, I knew she saw me and Jamar. What was worse was that we didn't know what she was going to do. Now I was here, watching her leave with my husband. Who knew what she had said to him? She could have told him everything just to be the spiteful bitch that she was.

I peeled off into the streets. I was doing highway speeds in residential neighborhoods. I just couldn't calm down. What did she tell him? What did he say? Was she smiling while she said it? Did she take pictures of us and we didn't see her? She had looked so shock to see us together. Who knew what she was going to do.

When I got home, I ran to my room. I started to pace back and forth. I was so glad that my mother had my daughter. The last thing I needed her to see was her mother panicking. I sighed and shook my head. This whole thing was getting more and more dramatic. This was not something I had planned at all.

The three hard knocks at my door sent jolts all through my body. I was so uneasy. It had to be Darius. He was pissed off because that bitch Jayla had told him everything. I bet you she'd twisted the story and added new shit to the story. I bet when she'd told it, she'd been gloating and bragging. I hoped I got the satisfaction of putting that bitch in her place one day.

I tiptoed to the door and looked out the window. I peeked out to see if I could see who was at the door. I was so relieved to see that it was Jamar.

"Yes!" I snatched the door wide open and pulled him in. "I'm so glad to see you."

"Babe, what's going on?" he asked me. "You look so worried." He held me close.

"I'm going crazy."

"What's worrying you?"

"Well how about the fact that the little slut saw us together?" I reminded him. "Who knows what that little bitch said to him? She could have turned this thing into something else."

"I know." He sighed. "But right now it's out of our hands. I called Darius and he was with Jayla."

"I already know that because I was spying on them. He took her to a little restaurant over in Buckhead." I crossed my arms. "I can't believe what's going on. Or is it that I don't know what's going on? This is going to drive me crazy." I turned to Jamar. "Did you talk to our friend?"

"Who?" He looked at me, confused.

"Our *friend*," I emphasized. "You know what I mean when I say that, don't you?" I gave him a knowing look. He soon caught on, because his eyes opened wide.

"Oh yeah, our *friend*. No. I didn't talk to the friend yet."

"Shit. Me neither." I felt my anxiety kick up a notch. "What if she told him? What if she told him what she saw?"

I rocked back and forth in place. I gave myself a tight hug. I was trying to calm down, but just thinking of what Jayla might have told him was driving me even more insane.

"You said that you talked to Darius tonight?" I remembered him saying it earlier.

"Just briefly."

"What did he say?"

"Nothing really. All he told me was that he was out with her."

"Did he sound mad?"

"No. He sounded pretty much the same. If she told him, I doubt he would have been that cool, calm, and collected."

"So far all we know is that she didn't tell him by the time you called him. I wonder if that means that she is telling him now." I grabbed myself tighter.

"What if I talk to him?" he suggested. "What if I try to find out?"

Jamar may have come up with the idea, but he was clearly nervous. He was panicking more than me. I now saw that by falling apart, we were both becoming unraveled. I had to get myself together. I used to deal with crises all the time when I was a real estate agent. I didn't crumble then, and I was not going to do that now. I took a deep breath and blew out all of my fears.

"What are you going to do?"

"I'm just going to talk to him and see what he knows."

"And how are you going to do that? You can't just pop up and say anything. You have to have a plan."

"I don't know what I'm doing," he said nervously. "I'm just coming up with this as I go along." He started to look scared. "Oh shit."

"What is it?"

"What are we going to do when he finds out?"

"If he finds out," I corrected him. "Let's not speak that into existence. Let us try to control what we can. You came up with a pretty decent plan. You go to talk to Darius and see what you can find out. If you find out that she didn't tell him by tomorrow, she probably won't, or maybe she's waiting it out. We just have to stick to the plan, all of our plans."

"But what if it ruins our chances?" he added.

"What?" Now I was the one who was confused. "What are you talking about now?"

"What if he finds out? Do you know that means we can't be together? We can't live the life that we want. We have plans to be together, Shenice. I need to know that we will be together at the end of all of this." He was getting even antsier.

"Jamar...I need you to calm down. You're not thinking right now. We can't get carried away. We're letting ourselves down by panicking like this." I was getting slightly annoyed with his attitude.

"And what about the big opportunity?" He was even more nervous.

"Babe," I slightly snapped at him, "I said it will be fine."

"Ok." He started to regain his composure.

"Do you trust me?"

"Yes?"

"Do you love me?"

"Yes." He smiled and looked like his old self.

"Then believe me when I say that everything is going to be fine. I have everything under control." I felt his body ease up, and he nodded his head.

Chapter 5

Darius

The new marketing campaign that Jamar came up with was genius. We were going to use social media to market the business. We were even now thinking of developing our own mobile application. Now when residents of Georgia wanted to do anything that dealt with real estate, they could just download an app. Everything was on the internet and on smartphones. We were simply keeping up with the times.

"Jamar..." I started. "You are a genius." I patted his back. He was crashing in my office, typing crazy fast on his laptop.

"I know I'm a genius. It's nice to know that you have finally gotten on board." He chuckled.

"But this whole thing with using social media, it's great. What made you come up with it?"

"I just thought about the young kid who came up with Facebook. A lot of the newest millionaires are young guys who came up with something new in social media. A lot of them live on this technology. It only made sense."

"I tell you, you and I are a great team. With me being the best real estate agent on the East Coast and your marketing ideas, we're gonna take this whole shit over." I laughed. "I can see us taking it over for real. You know, once this is really successful, we can open another branch."

"I like the sound of that."

"Get some young blood in this office."

"I like the sound of that." He reached up and we exchanged hands.

"This is the start of something good."

I got back to typing. I sensed something strange in Jamar. He was happy, but he was a bit reserved. Usually when I told him something great about himself, he wouldn't stop talking about it. This dude knew how to drain a compliment. I'd just given him a huge one, and he'd barely done anything with it.

"Hey bro, you cool?" I asked as I saw him drifting into space. "You're just staring away and daydreaming," I informed him. "That's not like you at all."

"I know, just a lot on my mind."

"You want to talk about it?" I asked.

"Nah, not really," he told me, and it felt off, because we could talk about almost anything.

"Damn. What could be so bad that you can't even tell your boy?"

He slit his eyes at me and looked at me suspiciously.

"What do you mean by that?"

"I'm just saying that you can tell me anything and everything. I've never had you not tell me a story. We always go back and forth looking for advice. I just want to repay you back for all the advice you've given me."

"How about we finish up here at work, wrap it up a little bit early, and head out to the bar."

"Now you're speaking my language." I laughed. "That sounds like a plan."

After work we headed to a local bar. I didn't know why I kept pounding back the drinks, but after four shots, I felt like the room was spinning. Jamar looked at me like I was a pitiful fool. I started to tell him about Shenice and Jayla. He asked me a million questions I wasn't ready to hear.

"Not now. Not this. The room is spinning." I held on to my head.

"Just tell me what it is about Jayla."

"This again?" I propped myself up on my elbow. "I thought I already told you about this."

"You like to talk when you're drunk." He laughed. "Now tell me about Jayla."

"Jayla is sexy, cool, and she doesn't nag me to death. Shenice is a fucking headache. As much as she's done for me, she got to keep pestering me."

"And you have no feelings for Shenice?"

"I love Shenice. You know what she's done for me. I'm always gonna be happy about that, but I can't help but feel like I should be with both of them."

"Both of them? Or one of them?"

"I could see myself with her," I muttered with my head resting against the counter of the bar. The bartender handed me another shot glass. I gulped it down, and I could see from the corner of my eye Jamar shaking his head.

"Slow down on the drinks," he advised me, but I wasn't listening. I needed something to help me. I was stressing out, and the drinks were helping out a little bit. He started laughing, looking at me struggle to get up. "Who do you see yourself with, Darius?" He was still laughing. "Be with who? Are you talking about Jayla? She cute and all, but you have a wife, remember," he mumbled to me as he grabbed his drink. He took a sip of it and looked back at me.

"I love my wife," I confessed, slurring because of all of the alcohol I was drinking. "I love Jayla too," I added. "What if I can't choose?" I asked him, still leaning on the counter for support. "I can just have both, right?"

My friend looked at me, shaking his head. I guess I looked pretty bad and pathetic right now. I caught a glimpse of myself in the mirror. I was in a pretty pitiful state.

"What can I tell you, man? There is no such thing as having them both!" He told me what I already suspected. "You can either have one or the other, but you can't have them both."

"Yes, I can. I can have them both!" I argued. "Why can't I? They both want me, and I want the both of them. So by those rules, I can have them both," I slurred some more and signaled for another drink. When I saw the bartender look over at Jamar, shaking her head, I knew that I was in worse shape that I thought.

"What do you want?" Jamar questioned me as he sipped his drink. He gave a motion to the bartender, letting her know that she should cut me off.

"What do I want?"

"Yeah. What do you want from them? There has to be something one of them is giving you that the other isn't."

"Yeah?"

"So what is it?"

"I don't know."

"What is it about Jayla?"

"She cute."

"I know." He sighed. "But what else about her?"

"She's got a good head on her shoulders, she's strong, she's all about her family, and the sex." I sat up straight. "It's the best."

"And Shenice isn't?"

"I'm not saying that she isn't, but Jayla is something else when it comes to fucking." I smiled.

"And what about Shenice?"

"That's my wife, that's the mother of my child, and without her, I don't know where I would be. She pretty much gave me my career. She saw something in me that I didn't even know was there. I'm grateful to her."

"Being grateful and being in love are two different things."

"I know."

"And you should be fair to these ladies."

"I know." I started to get more annoyed.

"And one of these days you are going to have to choose."

"I know! I know! I fucking know!" I yelled.

The whole bar got quiet. Everyone was staring at me, and I saw the bartender watching us. I ran my hand over my low-cut fade. I sighed and then breathed in hard.

"My fault," I apologized. I didn't mean to snap at Jamar, but he was asking too many fucking questions. The worst part about his fucking questions was that I didn't have the answers to them.

"It's alright." He took a deep breath while he settled the check. "I guess this shit is really stressing you out."

"It is."

"Well how about for now, you just do you." He stood up.

"What you mean?" I tried to stand, but I couldn't at the moment. Being the good friend that he was, Jamar helped me up.

"Al right, alright." He laughed as we made our way to the door. "You can have both, for now. Just watch out though. One of them is going to get tired of you. I can see it already."

I thought about what he said and shook my head. We left the bar.

"You know what?" he asked me right outside the bar. "I forgot to ask you something."

"That's impossible." I laughed and almost fell. "You were like a damn journalist in there. How is it that you even have any questions left?"

"Just a few more and then I can leave you with your soon-to-come hangover."

"What is it?" I leaned against the wall for support.

"Do you want to be with one more than the other? I know you just said that you can have both, but could you see yourself with one more than the other?" he asked. I thought about what he said.

"Jayla" was my answer. "Something is just telling me to be with Jayla. I know that's going to be messy because I left out some things, but I want to be with Jayla." I felt the truth pouring out of me. You know what they say happens when you drink.

"Cool." He nodded his head. "Speaking about Jayla, how was your date the other night?"

"It was nice."

"Did anything happen?" he questioned.

"Anything like what?"

"Like did she act weird?"

"Act weird?" I scrunched up my face. "Well now that you mention it, she was a little off."

Jamar looked a little worried, or was that all the drinks I'd had? I honestly couldn't tell the difference anymore. I should have slowed up on the liquor.

"How was she off?" he quizzed me again.

"She just seemed distant. Or it seemed like she had something to say. She kept trying to say something, but then she stopped herself. It was kind of strange."

"What did she say when you asked her?"

"She said that she was just tired from work."

"You believe her?"

"Yeah, I believe her. Jayla is the type that if she had something to say to me, she would have said it. If she tells me that her work is stressing her out, I believe her."

"Oh." He looked so relieved.

"You look happier to hear that news than me." I laughed out loud.

"I'm just looking out for my boy." He patted me on the back.

Jamar looked happy to hear that me and Jayla were on track. It seemed like as soon as he heard me tell him that everything was okay, he felt fine. That was what good friendship was. He was my brother. When I felt pain, he felt pain, and I guess when everything was going well for me, he felt the same.

"So, where to now?' I asked him.

"You need to get into a cab and head to a hotel."

"A hotel? Why not go home?"

"You're a mess," he told me, looking me up and down. I felt myself staggering and leaning over. He was right. I felt sick, and I didn't want to be around my family like this at all.

"You may have a point." I stood up straight. I used my phone to call a cab.

While we waited, we talked more about work. I was so glad about how great the company was doing. Jamar's plans and my ambitions were paying off.

"I can't wait for the new promotions for the company to come out. I'm so excited about that." I was feeling a bit better, but not enough to drive or go home. My head was starting to pound, and I was so ready to go to sleep. I was going to hit that hotel bed so hard, I might not wake up for days.

"I know what you mean. I really can't wait for the app to come out. Once it comes out and people download it, we will have a whole new client base. We are going to have a whole bunch of new clients that we've never had before."

"It's going to be more crazy clients too." I laughed a bit, remembering the lady I'd told Jayla about.

"But also a lot more money too," Jamar pointed out.

"I like the sound of that." I laughed. I steadied myself a bit more. "You know what we should do?"

"What's that?" He was holding on to my car keys and tossing them in the air.

"We should throw a launch party."

"That's a good idea. It will be another great way to meet clients and have a buzz about our business." He smiled and nodded his head. "I will have to get on that."

"Like I told you earlier, there is no better team than me and you." I shook his hand. He looked a little sad, but then he smiled.

"What can I say? You're like a brother to me."

The cab came and he helped me into it. He closed the door behind me. I brought the window down.

"Are you going to drive my car back home?" I asked him as he walked over to my Benz.

"Yeah." He waved at me.

"I don't know what I'd do without you." I waved goodbye. He honked the car horn twice. I told the driver where to go, and before I knew it, I'd drifted off into a peaceful sleep.

Chapter 6

Trey

The loud rap music in my ears had me feeling like a rapper. I mean my lifestyle was pretty close to a rapper's: I had a lot of money and was often surrounded by beautiful women. I wasn't having the flashy cars and homes, though. I wasn't trying to be broke before my time. I worked too hard and put in too much work to go broke because I was trying to live like Jay Z. All my money had a purpose, and everything I bought had a meaning.

I took out my small notebook. I wrote down almost every cent of money I ever got. I never wrote how I got it or the people's names who gave it to me, but I did have my own system. I just wanted to make sure that every cent I had was accounted for. When I gave out product to my boys, I made sure that they sold every ounce and gram. I didn't play that mess. I haven't had to beat down on one of my workers in a long time. I did it once, and from there on out, people respected me or feared me. I didn't care to be honest. As long as they kept the money coming in, I couldn't care less about that. I just got my work done, got the money, and made sure that everyone around me never starved.

"Trey." My boss's voice was low, but that was only because of the loud music in my ears. I turned it down and pulled the headphones out of my ears. "You going to go deaf listening to music that loud." He laughed.

"My mom used to always say that." I laughed. "She used to say that one day I'm going to wake up and not hear anything. She was always worried about me going deaf."

"Well she's right." He walked in and sat in one of my chairs. "You know how long I was yelling at you? Now what if I was someone coming up in here ready to shoot you?"

"Then that guy should come in here blasting, because the second I see him, he's dead."

"And what if I was the police?" He grinned at me.

"Then I need to see a warrant first and speak to my lawyer pronto. And all my things are locked up and better be listed on the warrant."

"I've taught you well." He nodded his head. "I don't know if I can tell you this enough times, but I'm proud of you. You are not one of my best workers; you are the best worker I have." He got into his bragging mode. "Everything I put out in front of you, you accomplish with great results. You know you are who I model the next generation after? If I meet some young guy and he doesn't remind me of you, I don't do any business with him, period."

"For real?" I sat up completely straight. "That's a good look."

"And you are good business. Every mission I send you out on, you get it. I just wanted to tell you to keep up the good work."

"No problem." I stood up and shook his hand.

"And something else."

He reached into his pocket and pulled out a thick yellow envelope. I didn't have to be psychic to guess what was in there. I just took it and shook his hand again.

"I appreciate this," I told him. "Thank you."

"It's nothing but love." He grabbed my shoulder firmly.

"I just want to say thanks for taking a chance on me when you first met me. I know it couldn't have been easy."

"It wasn't." He laughed. "But you never made me regret the decision." He let go of me. "I'm going to go now. You keep it up," he told me.

"I'll be around later to drop off some more money to you. We are making a lot of money out there. I think we can add a few more drips and triple up our money."

"Always about the money," he added before he left. "That's why I like you." He laughed. "Don't forget what I told you about the loud music. Don't play it too loud in your ears. You might get something worse than being deaf," he warned me on his way out.

He was gone, and it didn't take long for me to count the money in the envelope. It was nothing but $100 bills. They were all so crisp and neat, so I knew that he recently got it. When I finished counting them all, I saw that he'd given me $10,000 in cash. I nodded my head in approval. I got up and locked the door. My boss was right about one thing: I was slipping up. I had never been so relaxed like that before. My door was always locked. He was right to say that he could have been anybody. If somebody was dumb enough to run up in the room while I had my headphones on, I would have been dead. I wouldn't even have heard them coming.

I got my backpack and put the money in a different bag. Just when I was about to close my bag, I saw the picture. I had a target to eliminate. I was paid by that go-getter Shenice. Like my boss said, I always got the job done. I pulled out the rest of the papers. I had some more planning to do. Since I was getting rid of this person, it had to be perfect, flawless. I didn't need to fuck up at all. I never made mistakes before, and I wasn't planning to with this job. Shenice had paid me for a job well done, and that's what she was going to get. I had a reputation, and I wasn't going to ruin it.

I finished up the plans and decided that it was time to head home. I pulled out my cell and texted my driver one word: home. Two minutes later, I heard him honking the horn downstairs. I made it down and gave him $500 out of the bonus my boss just gave me.

"What is this for?" he asked.

"You always loyal," I told him. "You do your job, and you do a good one at that. Don't think I'm not going to pay you your regular either. What I just gave you was just a little extra to show you my appreciation."

"That's a good look. I appreciate that." He put the money away.

"Nah, you earned that," I told him, and I meant every word of it. With this driver behind the wheel, I never got into any bullshit at all. Even when we did get pulled over by the police, he always found a way to get us out of it. He didn't say anything else. He just nodded at me. He then pulled off and we started to make it back to my crib.

As always, the first thing I did when I got home was take a shower. It had been a long day, and it was my way of winding down. Once that warm water hit me, my muscles got all loose. I was no longer tense. Sometimes I would think it would be nice to have a female to help me ease a little bit more tension, but then I thought about all the money I would lose to keep her happy, and it was not worth it. If I got that tense, I'd just go to the strip club and fuck the shit out of a stripper. A lot of them would do anything for the money, and I happened to have a lot.

I started to get dressed. After I finished, I opened my backpack and took out all the money. I separated what was mine and what was for the business. I put the business money in one safe and I put my money in another. My personal safe was in the back of my closet while the business safe was under the bed. When I finished putting all the money away, I saw a piece of paper peeking out of the backpack. I picked it up and saw that it was the picture of my target. I shook my head. I'd done a lot of work, but I'd never thought this would be something I would feel. I'd never felt hesitant about completing a task.

Usually when I got an assignment, I do it and ask no questions. That was what my boss liked about me. He told me to sell drugs, and I'd have it done. He told me to beat someone down, and I was stomping them out. Whatever the job called for, I did it. But now looking at this picture, I couldn't help but feel a little sorry for them. This person won't even see it coming. This person didn't even know that I was planning out their death right now. All they knew was that one day everything was going to seem normal, and the next thing they knew...lights out

I looked at their picture some more and then I remembered the woman who had hired me, Shenice. There was a beautiful woman who was determined to get rid of this person. She had to really hate them if she went and found me. She wanted them off the face of the earth, and that was what I had to do. She'd hired me for a job, and even if I did feel some type of way, I had to do what I had to do. This is how the business goes. Every now and then everyone had to do something that they didn't completely agree with for money. Some people didn't know how to handle it. Luckily I did. I crumpled the picture up and threw it in the waste basket. It went in without a problem. This person had to be erased.

It was finally the big day. Today was the day I had to kill my target. I stretched my way out of bed. I hopped in the shower and let the warm water hit me. I would usually take my time a little, but I had no time to spare. I had work to do. I got dressed and ready. I had already gone over my plan a million times. Nothing was going to mess me up. Everything was going to be precise and this person was going to be gone. Just the other day I got the weapons that I needed. My regular guy came and dropped them off.

"Now these guns right here"—he held them up— "they will turn niggas into dust." He laughed. Ronald was his name, and he had a thing for weapons. He could get his hands on almost any weapon you could think of. He used to joke that he was still trying to get a tank.

I grabbed the weapon Ronald had given me another day. It was clean and brand new. Of course the serial number was filed out, but I didn't care.

Ronald always made sure the guns had no bodies on them. If there was going to be anyone using this gun to kill people, it was going to be me. I used them, did my dirt, and give them back to him. Ronald always found some way to get rid of guns. I suspected that he sold them to other people who lived out of state, but I didn't care. As long as I finished my job and put this person down for a dirt nap, it didn't matter. Luckily Ronald was like me; he was very particular about his business. He wasn't sloppy, because he and I both knew that sloppiness brought in mistakes.

I texted my driver only one word: time. I didn't wait for him upstairs. I came downstairs. I didn't need him honking. I saw him pull up, and he nodded his head at me.

"Where to?"

"You remember that address I gave you the other day?"

"Yes," he answered. He was always on his game. "You want to head out there."

"Yeah, but be about half a block down. I just want to be careful." I leaned back into the seat. I could only plan so much to be perfect, but I even planned for mistakes or things to go wrong. I was as efficient as they came.

The car started to move. I looked out the window and watched the neighborhoods change. There was so much to do, and I had to make sure it was perfect. I noticed that we were getting close to the location. I saw an offside road that was pretty close.

"Ok, right here," I told him. I saw the green car parked there. "Toss me the keys," I demanded. He opened the visor flap and threw me the car keys.

"You sure you don't want me to go with you?" my driver asked me. "I would feel better if I was around."

"I appreciate that, but you know that I can take care of myself," I reminded him. "You got your gun and phone with you?"

"At all times."

"Good. If anything is wrong, I'll text you a question mark. You have the address. You come in there blasting if you have to, but you just remember to get me the fuck out." He nodded his head. "It shouldn't go down like that though." I hesitated. "I'm going to do what I have to do, bring the car back, and then you drive the green car away to the chop shop."

"Not a problem."

I hopped out of the all-black truck. I closed the door behind me and went into the ordinary green car. It was just a plain, four-door car. It wasn't flashy or anything. There wasn't any rims or anything like that. All it had were slightly tinted windows, which made it great. I needed something that was going to blend in with the environment. I didn't need something that was going to stick out and that people would stop and stare at. What made this car even more perfect was that the shade of green was so dark, you didn't know if it was dark blue, dark green, or black. So on the off chance anyone saw it, there would be conflicting reports on the color of the car.

I got in the car and started the engine. I began driving toward the home of my target. I tapped the car horn twice. My driver tapped his once and I was gone. I gripped the gun in my gloved hand.

"Time to make shit happen," I told myself, and I was on my way.

~~~

**Find out what happens next in
His Dirty Secret Book 5! Available Now!**

His Dirty Secret 5:

Shenice realizes that she may have bit off more than she could chew, especially when her perfectly concocted plan takes a sudden turn. Jayla and Darius already have problems brewing in their lustful relationship, but they have no idea that they have something else they should be worried about. Something that could end it all for one of them.

Find out what happens next in part five of His Dirty Secret! Get Your Copy Today!

CPSIA information can be obtained at www.ICGtesting.com
Printed in the USA
LVOW10s1451070616

491590LV00014B/625/P